Tell Me About HEAVEN
...I Think I'm Forgetting

Written by Janet Clowes-Johnson
Illustrated by Catherine Reishus McLaughlin

Ideals Children's Books • Nashville, Tennessee
an imprint of Hambleton-Hill Publishing, Inc.

I would like to express my deepest love and gratitude to my Mom, my Dad, and my sister JoAnn... your love is my confidence.

And a special dedication to three of the greatest teachers ever: Mrs. Dorothy Davidson, my first-grade teacher who taught me to read; Mrs. Rosella Hall, the librarian who taught me my great love for books; and to Ms. Ernestine Yarborough, my fifth-grade teacher, who encouraged me to write creatively.—J.C.-J.

Foremost, I would like to thank our Heavenly Father, our Lord Jesus, and the Holy Spirit, for guidance and inspiration. Next, I feel honored to thank my parents, Emilie and Olaf Reishus, for the faith, diligence, and creativity in their lives. A special thank you to my husband, Scott, and our angel babies, Augustin, Connor, and Gabrielle, for your love and support. It was a joy to paint you for this book. My paintings are also in loving memory of my Granny, Kathleen Overby, and brother, Skip. Finally, I am grateful also to Janet for writing such a precious book, and to all the special children and adults who modeled for this book.—C.R.M.

Published by Ideals Children's Books
An imprint of Hambleton-Hill Publishing, Inc.
Nashville, Tennessee 37218

Library of Congress Cataloging-in-Publication Data
Clowes-Johnson, Janet, 1966-
Tell me about heaven—I think I'm forgetting/ by Janet Clowes-Johnson ; illustrated by Catherine Reishus McLaughlin. — 1st ed.
p. cm.
Summary: A boy seeks answers to his questions about Heaven from his baby brother, who he believes has just come from that celestial place.
ISBN 1-57102-100-0 (hardcover)
1. Heaven—Christianity—Juvenile literature. [1. Heaven.] I. McLaughlin, Catherine Reishus, ill. II. Title.
BT849.C56 1998
236'.24—dc20 96-38764
CIP
AC

The illustrations in this book were rendered using gouache and various brushes, including airbrush.
The text type is in Goudy.
The display type is in Cochin.

First Edition
10 9 8 7 6 5 4 3 2 1

Author's Note

There was once a story told to me of a little boy, only three-and-a-half years old, whose life was filled with all the ups and downs of parents facing life's problems. This little boy was determined to talk to his new baby brother . . . alone. After much urging and insistence and pleading, the parents agreed and left the two little fellows alone. But being curious parents they slipped back into their bedroom and eavesdropped over the nursery monitor. They heard their eldest son make his way to the crib, and then they heard him clearly say, "Tell me about Heaven. I think I'm forgetting."

When I heard this story, I was filled with awe and amazement. In their newness of life, children still carry so much innocence and sweetness, that I began to wonder if it is possible for them to have some recollection of being in Heaven, of, perhaps, dancing with the angels.

I don't know where our souls are formed, whether it is here on earth or in heaven. This book is not intended to define what paradise is or to be fact; rather, it is a wondering, a wondering about our God, a wondering about the Greatest Creator of all time and space, who knits us together in the intimate seclusion of our mother's womb. Would he also design us with enough of a remembrance of a haven so rich and good that we yearn for that sweet perfection, just around the corner of our lifetime?

This book was inspired by that little boy who made me sit and wonder about that incredible somewhere beyond our wildest imaginings, that place where I will be going when I am finished here on Earth, and that place maybe from which I came.

Tell me about Heaven.

What color is Heaven?
Are there really streets of gold?

The great street of the city was of pure gold, like transparent glass.
Revelation 21:21b (NIV)

Are the clouds as soft as feather pillows?
Do they taste like marshmallows
. . . or is that cotton candy?

The heavens declare the glory
of God; the skies proclaim
the work of his hands.

Psalm 19:1 (NIV)

Does Jesus like to take long walks through the meadows of heaven?
Can you still hold his hand while you tiptoe under the stars?

He is the maker of the Bear and Orion, the Pleiades and the constellations of the south.

Job 9:9 (NIV)

Does Jesus ever talk about being a kid in the carpentry shop? or about the time he and Joseph made a jigsaw puzzle in the shape of a lamb?

Isn't this the carpenter's son?
Matthew 13:55 (NIV)

Are angel wings hard or soft? light or heavy?
Do they have different types of wings, like playtime wings or dress-up wings? Do the wings make rustling sounds when they move?

The sound of the wings of the cherubim could be heard as far away as the outer court, like the voice of God Almighty when he speaks.
Ezekiel 10:5 (NIV)

Do the angels come with their harps and play you a lullaby when you nap in the hammock by the rainbow?

And I heard a sound from heaven . . .
like that of harpists playing their harps.
Revelation 14:2 (NIV)

When a person on Earth does something good, do Jesus and all the angels stand up and cheer ?

Do not forget to entertain strangers,
for by doing so some people have
entertained angels without knowing it.
Hebrews 13:2 (NIV)

Is God's smile as wide as the galaxies?
What makes God giggle?

The Lord your God is with you, . . .
He will take great delight in you,
he will quiet you with his love;
he will rejoice over you with
singing.

Zephaniah 3:17 (NIV)

Can you go and sit in Jesus' lap whenever you need a hug?
Is he really the best friend I'll ever have?

Jesus said, "Let the little children come to me, and do not hinder them, for the kingdom of heaven belongs to such as these."
Matthew 19:14 (NIV)

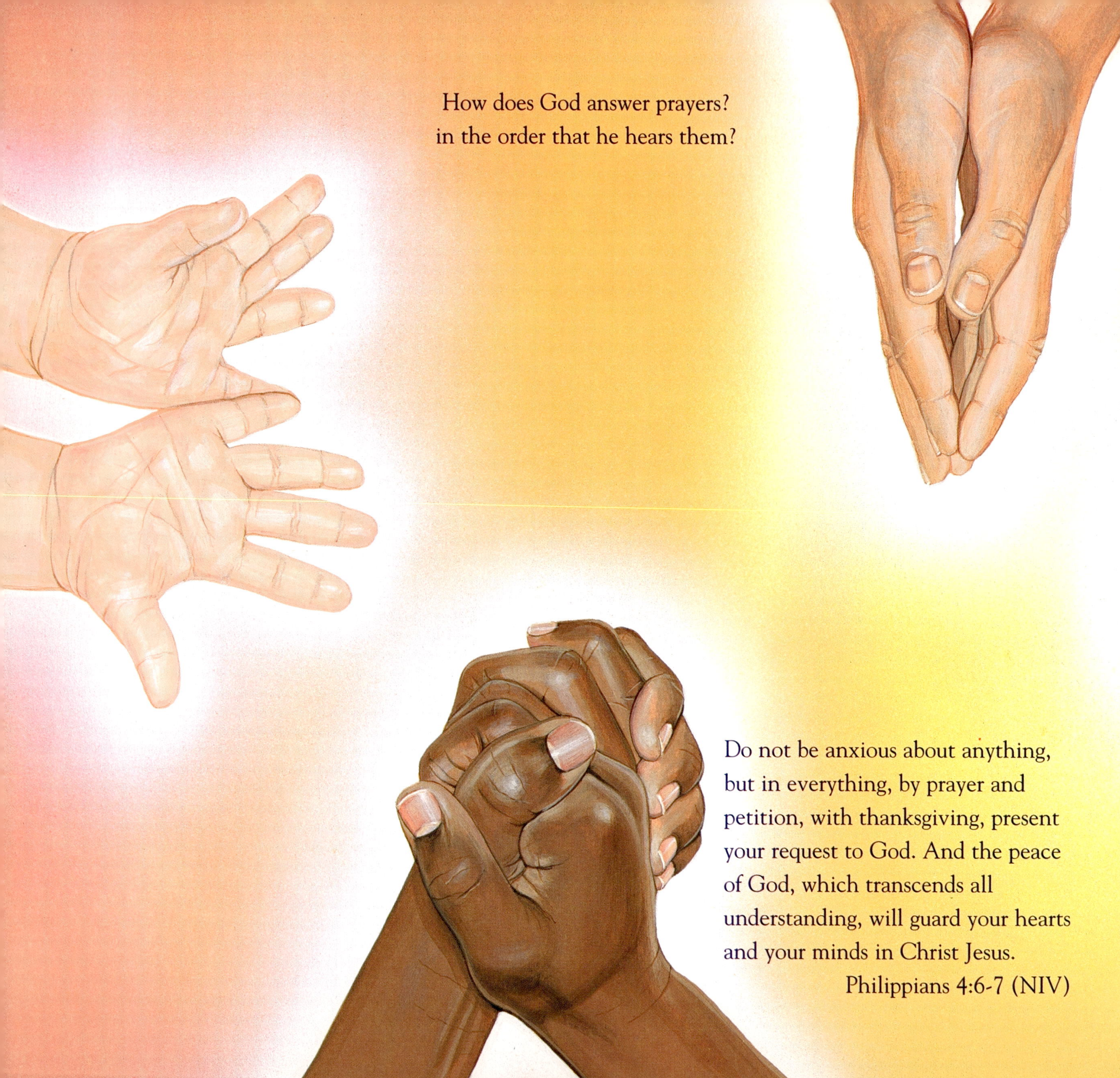

How does God answer prayers?
in the order that he hears them?

Do not be anxious about anything, but in everything, by prayer and petition, with thanksgiving, present your request to God. And the peace of God, which transcends all understanding, will guard your hearts and your minds in Christ Jesus.

Philippians 4:6-7 (NIV)

Will Jesus always watch over me?
Is he watching over me right now?

For he will command his angels concerning you to guard you in all your ways;
they will lift you up in their hands, so that you will not strike your foot against a stone.

Psalm 91:11–12 (NIV)

Is it true that no one ever gets scared in Heaven?
and no one ever cries?

And God shall wipe away all tears from their eyes; and there shall be no more death, neither sorrow, nor crying, neither shall there be any more pain: for the former things are passed away.

Revelation 21:4 (KJV)

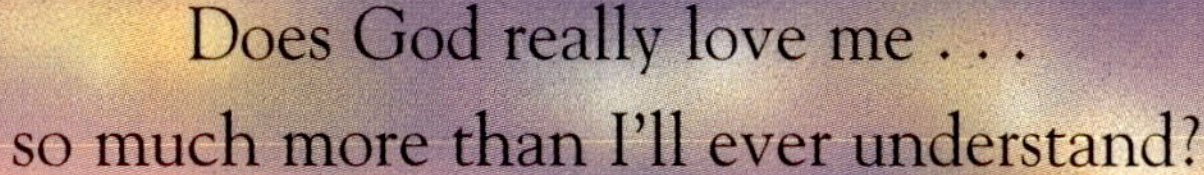

Does God really love me . . .
so much more than I'll ever understand?

For God so loved the world that he
gave his one and only Son.
John 3:16 (NIV)

Tell me about Heaven . . . I think I'm forgetting.